PART
OF
LIFE

MAYANK SINHA

BLUEROSE PUBLISHERS
India | U.K.

Copyright © Mayank Sinha 2024

All rights reserved by author. No part of this publication may be reproduced, stored in a retrieval system or transmitted in any form or by any means, electronic, mechanical, photocopying, recording or otherwise, without the prior permission of the author. Although every precaution has been taken to verify the accuracy of the information contained herein, the publisher assumes no responsibility for any errors or omissions. No liability is assumed for damages that may result from the use of information contained within.

BlueRose Publishers takes no responsibility for any damages, losses, or liabilities that may arise from the use or misuse of the information, products, or services provided in this publication.

For permissions requests or inquiries regarding this publication, please contact:

BLUEROSE PUBLISHERS
www.BlueRoseONE.com
info@bluerosepublishers.com
+91 8882 898 898
+4407342408967

ISBN: 978-93-5989-579-6

Cover design: Rishav Rai]
Typesetting: Rohit

First Edition: February 2024

Dedicated

*To all my mentors who
always had faith in me.*

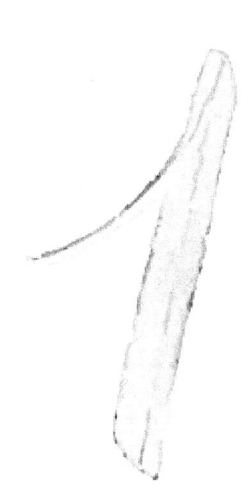

It was the winter of 2015. I finally got a chance to visit Bangalore. I have been in network marketing for almost a year now. This felt like a big break. It seemed to me like an open market, and I thought that it would be great if I got my nodes open over here. So, with one backpack and hope in my eyes, I took the 30-hour journey to my destination.

As the train halted, a cool breeze welcomed me. This was a new town for me. Completely unchartered territory. I was nervous yet excited to find out what this place had in store for me.

My sister, Nisha, was in college. I had planned to meet her and show her the marketing plan. What I was selling was fairly simple: it was a computer course and holiday package, along with the prospect of creating a network of people under you and earning an income on the side.

By the time I reached Nisha's college campus, it had gotten late. I was greeted by my sister. She then brought two of her friends (Sneha and Awa) for the mini-presentation that I was about to give. This was the first time that I saw her. "Hi, I am Sneha," she said. She had this childlike smile on her face that I noticed at first. Her hair was tied in a ponytail, and she was wearing a dark blue top with white polka dots and blue jeans. There was no makeup on her, but she was still pretty.

By the time I got to meet her, I couldn't find any place to sit down and give the presentation, so I just postponed it for the next day. While going back to my hotel room, I was nervous about the presentation, yet I could remember her face clearly.

The next day, I got my paper and pen ready. And headed for my destination. After an hour of commuting, I was there. This time, I was greeted by my sister and Sneha. Something in Sneha seemed new, as I could tell. For some reason, she was smiling too much, and her face had this glow that I had not seen yesterday. I didn't think much of it and went on to give my presentation. It was on paper, and I tried to present it to the best of my knowledge.

After the presentation, Nisha, Sneha, Awa, and I decided to go to the nearby food court named Ascendas. We had pizza and cold drinks. It was a fun talk about the prospects of the business opportunity that I was offering. They seemed interested in my offer.

While returning from Ascendas, I started to have a discussion with Sneha and didn't realise when we started walking together while leaving the other two behind. I stopped when I heard giggles coming from behind. It was Nisha and Awa smiling from ear to ear.

But it didn't matter much, as I was having a great conversation. I don't know what I felt when I saw her every time; it just felt good to be around her. I escorted her to the campus, and then we sat on the staircase for a chat.

This was the first time that I realised how amazing she looked. She was wearing a white top with blue patterns and blue jeans. Her hair was open and shifted to one side, revealing her gorgeous neck. Her hair looked like an extension of the night sky, and her face was in complete contrast to it. Her skin looked golden as the porch light reflected off of it. Her eyes looked like a mystical forest surrounded by fog. I don't recall what we talked about since I was transfixed by her voice and kept getting lost in her eyes whenever she glanced at me. All I know is that it felt right. Amidst all the feelings of nervousness and butterflies in my stomach, I knew one thing: it felt right to be there with her. And I think she sensed it too. We talked, but then I had to leave. I kept this memory of her and headed back to college.

While travelling back to my college. I could see her face flashing in front of me. Those eyes and that smile were all that I dreamed of. I didn't know what it was that I felt, as this had never happened to me before. But it felt nice; everything around me seemed to be in a good mood.

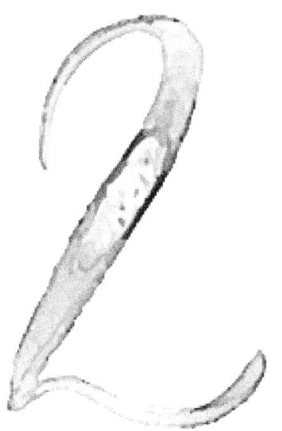

A week passed, and then a month. After that beautiful encounter with this girl, whom I met only once in my life, I still couldn't stop thinking about her. We didn't talk at all. We lived 1000 km apart. And so there was no chance of us just visiting each other to talk again. I had no way of contacting her other than through my sister. I finally decided to go for it.

It was the 4th of January, 2016. It was her birthday. I decided this was the best way to reach her and start a conversation. It was surprising to me that somehow the spark that I felt on that day was still there. And so our conversations began. We talked daily and found out that we had so many similarities. We had the same favourite colour. We liked the same food. And coincidentally, we preferred to listen to old songs before sleeping. I was having the best time of my life. I took the moment to propose to her. She said yes. And then, my joy knew no bounds.

Our relationship was long-distance, but I was ready to make it work out. I was prepared in my mind for it. I had thought of it many times. It was clear in my mind that I wanted to make it work out, and I was going to put all my effort into it.

Until today, whenever I look back, I am still unable to find a reason or an explanation as to what was in her that made me so fond of her. I just don't know. For a person with whom you have met only once, that person becomes an integral part of your life, so much so that you are afraid to lose them. And having so much affection and care for them to the point that their bad day spoils yours was a very new and unknown concept to me. It had never happened to me before. But even then, it just felt worth the effort. She felt worth the effort.

Our relationship was both exciting and yet subtle. We talked as if we had known each other for years. Sometimes even I was surprised at how we managed to get to know each other and understand each other so well in such a short time. We had our arguments and fights, which usually ended with us apologising to each other. (Mostly, it was me apologising.)

For some reason, this relationship mattered. It was the first time that I felt anything like this. And she just became very important to me. It didn't matter to me how quickly this relationship was pacing or in which direction. I was just there with all of it. I just wanted to make it work out. And I guess maybe too much.

Almost a year had passed since this dream of a relationship. Every day I woke up to a "Good morning, handsome" message. And most of the nights went by when she would fall asleep while talking to me. We couldn't meet daily. But this was enough. To be able to fall asleep next to each other on call was our way of having intimacy in the relationship. She could sense whenever I was upset and would just ring me up to see if I was okay. I, too, had this intuition about her and would know when she was sad or just upset. My calling her at those times made her happy too.

From my point of view, everything seemed fine. I had a girlfriend whom I would cherish for the rest of my upcoming days. I was happy.

Now that I look back, I realise that most of the time, when we are trying to take care of our loved ones or trying to associate our emotional selves with them, we tend to forget that they are individuals as well. And they might have their own opinions and outlooks on the relationship. We become so fascinated by the prospect of having this one person in our lives that we tend to forget or overlook the possibility that they might be on a different page than us in the relationship. We all have a world of our own in our minds; the problem starts when we start imposing this utopia on our significant other. And I guess this is what happened to me.

It was the 13th of February. I was excited for the next day. I had some plans in my mind and some gifts that I had planned to give to my beloved Sneha. I was planning to make it a special Valentine's Day for us, as it would be our first.

That night, I got a call from Nisha. Her tone seemed tense and sad. I was not sure why she was in such a mood.

So I asked, "Hey, is everything okay?".

"Actually, no, I have to talk to you about Sneha," she replied.

"Yeah, sure, tell me," I said.

"Ah well, she has just reached out to me, saying that she doesn't want this relationship anymore; she just wants you both to be only friends," she said.

"Wait!" I fumbled.

"Yeah, she says that she doesn't feel the same for you, and that is why she chose to say it through me, as she doesn't want to hurt your feelings," she replied.

My heart just fell into my stomach. I did not know how to feel or react. Everything that I had hoped for or planned had just come to an end. Just like that. I was so shaken that I couldn't say anything for a minute.

"Give her the phone," I said.

"Hello Rohit..." Her voice was enough to bring me back to my senses. All my dream castles with her now just started to crumble and be washed out in the flood of my tears.

"Are you ok?" she asked again.

"Yeah," I replied, trying to control my tears and snobs. "Did I do something wrong?" I asked.

"No, nothing," she said.

"Then why are you doing this? I am sorry, Pari (the nickname I gave her)," I said.

"Don't be Rohit; it's not your fault. It's just that I don't feel that it'll work out; I don't feel for you the same way anymore. I am sorry, she replied.

There were some things that I said after that, but it's all hazy now. I was by then drenched in tears, and this had wrecked my emotions very badly. I just remember myself crying that night standing in 15-degree Celsius on the 2nd floor of my hostel balcony, in a T-shirt whose arms had been drenched in my tears. The wind was blowing and was chilling, but it did not affect me. I just stood there, numb and blank. Tears kept flowing for some reason, and the night only got darker, colder, and quieter.

The last memory of that night I have is that I went to the bathroom to wash my face so that my roommate wouldn't find out that I was crying. Then, reaching my room and sliding into my blanket,.

Muffling my sound with my pillow and then crying myself to sleep.

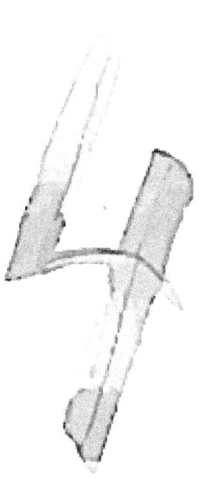

You know time doesn't give a shit about how you feel. It keeps moving on. And so the sun rose the next day. It was a holiday at our college. I woke up, but my head felt heavy and I felt dizzy, so I slept again. I didn't take a bath or have breakfast. Just lay flat on my bed, like a corpse. There were too many things going on in my mind—her voice, the things she said. The moments that we had kept flashing in front of my eyes, like a never-ending movie. I was becoming numb to everything and didn't feel like talking, eating, or even moving.

15 February onwards were my midterms. Only God knows how I got through them. I kept drifting while writing my exams into a swirl of thoughts of what we could've been and what my life would've been with her. But somehow, the midterms passed.

I am not very good at handling emotions. I can't process them. And as the eldest child in an Indian middle-class family, in general, I am not even supposed to have them.

At that time, I had no one to talk to regarding this. Nisha is younger than me, and so I couldn't open up as much as I wanted to with her. Call it male ego or any other superiority complex shit, I don't care. It's just how I am. It's difficult for me to open up emotionally to people. Sneha's thoughts kept flashing in front of me. It was driving me crazy.

So, I did what I was best at doing. I shut everything off. My emotions, my feelings, everything. I stopped my conversations with people, switched my smartphone to a dumb one with minimal functionalities, and went off the grid in every way that I could. And I started to distract myself and keep myself busy with one thing or another. Just so that I can keep my sanity intact.

At first, it was really difficult. I kept thinking about Sneha. It was really difficult to keep my focus and not drift into her thoughts. It took weeks and months, but slowly I got the hang of it. And life seemed to be coming back on track. Did I still care for her? Yes, I did. Did I still want to fix things? Yes, I did.

Was I a stupid dumbass for thinking all this? Absolutely.

I call myself a dumbass now because, looking back, I realise that's what I was. But, to me, it was just a phase before I got to be with her again. I was 19 at the time; I guess this nonsense is expected at that age. Being a closed person as a teenager is really difficult, as having no one to share my feelings with started taking a toll. And when I started to try to handle my feelings on my own, I started to lose sight of right and wrong and had no clue where I was going with this handling stuff.

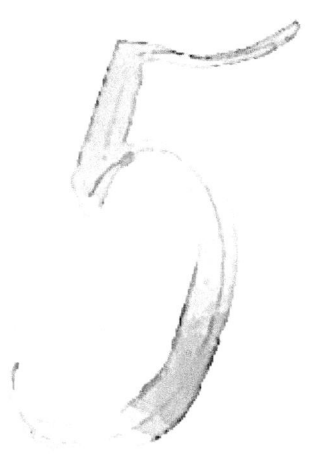

Around 7 months had passed in that phase. I was now slowly able to get a hold of myself. And being able to see the big picture of my life and career. I was now in my 3rd year of college and had to get serious about my studies as the campus placements would be starting by the end of the year.

But one night, as I was about to go to sleep, I got a call from an unknown number. The number seemed familiar, so I picked it up.

"Hello?" I said.

"Hi, how are you?" A reply came with a familiar voice.

"I am ok. Who is this again?" I asked just to confirm, even after knowing. "It's me. Sneha," she replied.

"Ah, hi," I said.

"I was just wondering about how you were; I haven't heard from you for a while. That's why I called; I figured that you wouldn't be having my number saved," she said.

"Oh, ah, it's nothing like that; actually, I just changed my mobile, so most of my contacts have been lost," I said.

"Oh, ok, you know what happened today in my college? I dressed up Awa as a mummy with tissue paper rolls," she said excitedly.

I guess this was the hope I had been looking for all along. And so it started again.

"Gussa mat ho g!!" (rough translation) Come on, man!! Don't be angry like that, was my go-to sentence whenever she used to get angry at me. And it had worked every single time, as this used to make her blush.

In our conversation, this tagline came up a few times. I could picture her blushing, her cheeks getting all red, and her voice getting softer on the earpiece while talking as she did.

"I missed you," she said.

"I missed you too," I replied.

We both wished each other good night, and then the call was over.

Our conversations had begun again. I was being extra careful this time not to screw things up. I suppose when we have affection for someone, we stretch our boundaries by giving them a second and often several opportunities. I felt at peace. Having her back in my life was the only thing that mattered to me.

I confessed that I still liked her. And I would want to be with her. She said that she liked me too and that I was more than a friend. But when it came to being in a relationship with me, she never gave a straight answer. There was always this uncertainty in her voice that bugged me.

Even though I liked and cared for her a lot, I started noticing that she never gave a clear answer when it came to being together. Ignoring this fact was slowly becoming harder for me. From my standpoint, she clearly knew that I liked her and was serious about being in a relationship with her. She even said she would love to be with me, but never said when that would be.

At this point in my life, I had started to come out of the hopeless romantic phase and started to see things for what they were. I still cared for her and liked her. But this uncertainty in her words started to seem fishy to me.

At first, I decided to give her some time, hoping that she would be able to make up her mind regarding it. In the next six months, we had many arguments regarding this. But still, I didn't get any clear answers from her.

So then, I decided to take matters into my own hands. I asked Nisha for help. I told Nisha to call me, put the phone down, and not tell Sneha that I was on call. And have a conversation with Sneha regarding how she felt about me. So, I get to listen firsthand to what she says. I had already told Nisha what Sneha told me about liking me and our arguments regarding being together. And so the call went. I sat on the other side of the call, listening intently.

"Sneha, I need to talk with you about Rohit," Nisha said. "Yeah, tell me," Sneha replied.

"What do you think about Rohit?" Nisha asked. "Rohit is a nice guy, caring, and funny," Sneha replied.

"Not that. I mean, do you have romantic feelings for him?" Nisha asked. "No, I do not," Sneha replied.

"So, you do not have any feelings for him?" Nisha asked. "No, I don't have any feelings for him at all," Sneha replied.

"But you have said to him that you like him, right?" Nisha asked. "Did Rohit tell you that?" Sneha said

"Yes, you know that he has feelings for you," Nisha replied. "Yes, I do," Sneha said.

"Then why did you say that you liked him then?" Nisha asked.

"I like him only as a friend, and he doesn't understand that," Sneha replied.

"He must have asked you about this before, whether you like him or not," Nisha asked.

"Yes, he did, but I said that I liked him so that he wouldn't go through all that again when we first broke up. You know how he becomes when he is hurt; he stops talking and all. I don't want him to be hurt and go through all that again," Sneha replied.

"Lying to him about your feelings even after knowing how he feels for you is also not going to make him happy or help him," Nisha said. I could sense the anger in her voice.

"Understand this, Sneha. When a boy has feelings for you and you say that you like him, he is only going to conclude that you have feelings for him too. You like him only as a friend, and nothing more won't even come in his dreams; forget about his thoughts, Nisha said, trying to keep herself calm.

"Hmm, ok," Sneha replied.

"So, just to be clear, you only like him as a friend and nothing more, right?" Nisha asked. "Yeah, right," Sneha replied.

And the call was over. I didn't know what to say or feel. I just kept quiet and stared out the window. It was a fine evening. The wind was slowly blowing and was trying hard to push the overgrown orange clouds.

That conversation was the final nail in the coffin. That was the day when the emotional attachment and trust that I had in Sneha were broken. I tried to wrap my head around the fact that she would do such a thing to me. I tried to understand her perspective as well, but I was mad at her for this. And I couldn't find a logical explanation for her actions. I just sat there, lost in my thoughts, looking at the sky and seeing the sky change colour. And not knowing how to feel or react or what to say or to whom.

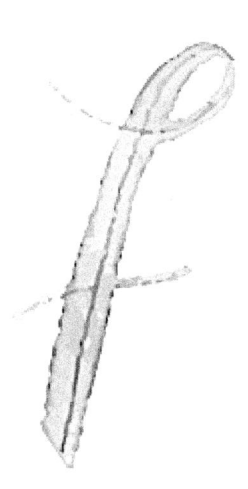

I woke up the next day, or rather, a part of me woke up to go to college. I had responsibilities on my shoulders that kept me going. After that day, I didn't ask or say anything to Sneha regarding the conversation; I just cut every connection with her as I knew I would not be able to control my temper and I would end up saying something hurtful to her.

Days slowly started to pass as the autumn leaves fell from the tree. I engrossed myself in my studies and started preparing for the campus placements. I boxed up all my emotions and feelings and kept them in some dark corner of my mind.

But there was this one thought that I couldn't help but notice. Even though I tried to ignore it and tried to even kill it or suppress it, it just wouldn't go away. It was that I missed Sneha; I still cared for her. Even after what had happened, I still cared for her a lot. I don't know why, but I just did. I hated myself for it, but those feelings were still there, and I did care for her despite everything that had happened.

I grew tired of trying to suppress and hide them, so I decided to take professional help as I was unable to understand these feelings that I had for her.

My psychiatrist, upon hearing the full story, asked me what I wanted to know.

"I just want to understand why I still care for her so much. And why do I keep missing her, despite everything that has happened? And even after killing every connection that I had with her and having not even spoken to her in months, why do I still miss her? And also, why am I not able to get out of this state of feeling helpless all the time?" I said.

"There is only one way to explain it. You have fallen in love with Sneha. That is why you are unable to stop caring for her. You can say that you are not attached to her anymore, but the feelings that you are describing are suggesting that in some way you still are, and it doesn't necessarily have to be romantic, but this feeling of care and affection towards another stems from attachment only. And as for your helplessness feeling, since in some way your feelings are suppressed, you are currently going through depression." she said.

"No, no, wait a minute, so you're saying that the girl who has never had any interest in me, and after what she has done despite knowing everything, I have still fallen in love with that girl! I don't believe you, I said.

"See, love doesn't need your permission to happen. It's a natural feeling. It happens when it does. And I am not saying that you have just fallen in love with her; you had fallen for her maybe a long time ago; it's just that you are realising it just now, that's all. And whether you believe it or not won't have any effect on it. It's still there. And you will have to understand that, she said.

"And now the final decision is up to you on how you want to face it," she added.

This conversation with my psychiatrist gave me a sense of closure. I finally knew what I was going through. But it also felt like a nightmare, as I had fallen in love with a person whom I was probably never going to meet again or even get to talk with again. And above all, she had clearly said that she had no interest in me. So it was already a lost battle for me.

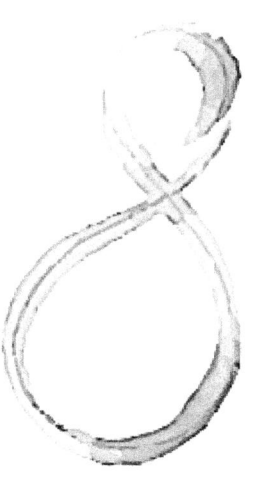

After this revelation, I went through several phases. The first phase was hating Sneha. I played the victim role in my mind and blamed everything on her. For my emotional attachment to her, I blamed her; for her coming into a relationship with me, I blamed her. I was just mad at her; for whatever I had faced and for everything that I had gone through, I blamed her for it. This phase lasted a couple of months. I realised that hating her was only taking a toll on me, and blaming her for everything was just not fair. And also, I slowly realised that you actually cannot hate a person you have fallen in love with. It's just not possible, because there is nothing known as unloving someone. Whether we like it or not, it's just a fact that we cannot unlove someone once we have loved them. We just learn to accept that they are not going to be a part of our lives, even though we want them to be, and then we just find someone whom we love even more.

So, now the second phase started, where I started hating myself. Because I had the face I saw every day in the mirror, and this guy won't have an excuse if I put all the blame on him. So I did that. I started finding faults in myself so that I could pinpoint the reason why I went wrong in the relationship. And what I could've done differently would have meant that the relationship would've survived. I started finding myself in this utopia of thoughts where I kept imagining what it could have been. If I had done one thing or the other differently, how would the relationship have turned out if we never broke up?. But slowly and gradually, this utopia started to lose its glitter as well. As reality dawned on me, this dream that I had been living in was never going to come true, and reality was far from it. And then I moved on to the next phase.

The third phase was a challenging one. Because in this phase, I learned to forgive myself. But before that, I had to go through the process of accepting that I was at fault in the first place. It took me months and months to go through this stage. But this stage was the one that changed me the most. My perception of life and love changed dramatically. I learned that love cannot be forced. And if it's being forced, then it's not love. I realised that a relationship consists of two people, and whether it works out or not in the end, the fruit or the fall of the relationship goes to only these two people.

I and Sneha were in a relationship. It didn't work out as I thought it would. So we are both responsible for it. I know and completely accept the fact that I was overly romantic in the relationship and maybe overwhelmed her with my feelings. But she was also there. If 90% of the fault was mine, I expected too much from the relationship. Then 10% of the fault also goes to her—that she wasn't ready to hold me when I was drifting into this pointless romanticism. And have me sit down and discuss the state of the relationship instead of just breaking up and leaving. So we are both to blame for the relationship.

To date, I do not know why or how I got so emotionally attached to her. Or why did I put so much effort into waiting for her or giving her a chance to clear things up between us? I guess maybe it was because I considered it to be my relationship and wanted to put in every effort so that, at the end of the day, I didn't have any regrets of any kind that the relationship didn't work out because I didn't put enough effort from my side.

But as I slowly accepted the fate of the relationship for what it was, I became a changed person. I was happy with who I was and started to live my life. My grades improved, and I got placed in a company. And soon I was working a job and taking steps towards becoming independent. Things seemed good now.

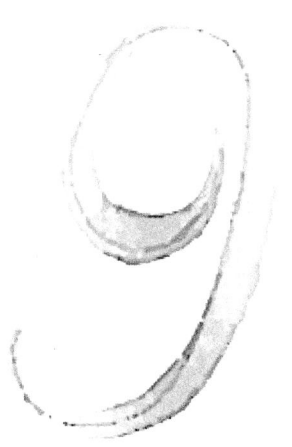

A year and a half had gone by. Sneha, for me now, was only a memory. A memory that just stayed with me. The thought of breaking up with her didn't fill me with remorse anymore. And the possibility of being with her doesn't excite or appeal to me now. All in all, I had made my peace with her. And myself, for that matter.

One evening in December 2018. I got a Facebook friend request. It was from Sneha. I was both surprised and confused as to what, or rather, why I was contacted all of a sudden by her. I started having a conversation with her:

Sneha: Hi

Me: Hi

Sneha: You are Nisha's brother, right?

Me: Yes... Don't you know me?.

Sneha: Oh yes, I think I remember meeting you once. But nothing followed that. So how is college going on?

Me: College? Hehe. I am now working for a company. I passed out long ago, don't you know?

Sneha: Oh, is that so? I'm actually sorry if I don't remember. One year ago, I had an accident and was diagnosed with epilepsy, and because of the medicine's side effects, I have lost most of my memories from my second year in college.

Me: What? Really? Do you want me to believe that? Come on, Sneha, don't fool around with me; we were in a relationship together. I know you better.

Sneha: Relationship? Which relationship? I don't remember anything like that. I don't even know you that well. Your face seemed familiar, and Nisha was on a mutual friend list, which is why I sent a request to you.

ME: What? Ok… I'll text you some time.

Sneha: ok.

I couldn't believe what I was reading. So I immediately called Nisha.

Nisha: Hello brother, so you do remember me after all; good to know.

Me: Yeah, yeah, listen, it's something important.

Nisha: Ok, tell me.

Me: I just got a friend request from Sneha. And so I started talking with her. But she is behaving very strangely. Saying that she doesn't remember me and stuff and that she doesn't even know me. Is this some kind of prank she is playing with me?.

Nisha: Actually, no, she is telling the truth. You must not be aware because you both were not in touch then. But last year, she had an accident. The autorickshaw she was travelling in slipped and turned over. And her head crashed against the metal frame of the rickshaw. After which, she was diagnosed with epilepsy. In that sense, she has lost most of her memories, and it's possible that she doesn't remember anything about you. So you will have to talk as if you are talking for the first time with her. Because if she stresses too much, then she might have a blackout.

Me: Really?

Nisha: Hmm, yes, I know it must be a lot to take in, but it is the truth.

Me: Hmm, ok. Just give me her number. I need to speak with her.

Nisha: ok.

While I waited for the contact number, I quickly googled about epilepsy. It turns out it is a neurological disorder in which the left side of the brain is not effectively able to communicate with the right side of the brain. And hence, as a result, the person suffering from it goes through blackouts or sudden seizures. It is not a fatal disease, but in most cases, it's incurable. These seizures are random, so the person needs to be careful about their surroundings, as seizures in an elevator, while climbing down the stairs, or in a place like that could result in seriously hurting the person.

My heart just sank, and my lower body became lifeless as I read it. My breathing had become heavier, and my throat got dry. My hands were shivering as I fumbled with my phone to dial her number. In that troubled state of mine, I somehow pressed the earpiece against my ear. With every dialer tone, my heart rose and skipped a beat.

Tring! Tring…! Click! Sneha- Hello?

Me: Hey... Hi... This is Rohit. Sneha: Oh yeah, hi.

Me: So how are you?

Sneha: I am okay. How are you?

Me: I am okay. I am now working for a company.

Sneha: Oh, that's nice. Congratulations.

Me: Thanks, so you really don't remember anything about me?

Sneha: I do remember some things about you, like that you are Nisha's brother. And you came to meet her once; then I met you too, I guess.

Me: Oh, yes, I did. Anything else?

Sneha: Ah, no sorry. There is nothing more than that. Did we used to know each other? Because it feels like I know you from somewhere, but I am not sure when.

Me: Hmm.. yeah, it seems we did get to know each other at one point in time.

My entire relationship with her and all the moments that I had with her, good or bad, Were flashing in front of me. They had all now lost meaning, as she didn't remember them at all. I thought that I had gained control over my emotions by now, but my voice and my eyes were suggesting otherwise.

Sneha: Oh, ok. So, like, how well did we know each other?

Me: Ah, actually, there was a time that you and I were in a relationship.

Sneha: What? You are joking, right? As far as I remember, I have always been single. Don't mess around with me now.

Me: Ah, yeah, actually, it is true; it's just that you don't remember it anymore. So… Ah, nevermind, it doesn't matter anymore; leave it. How… How are you doing now? Do you feel alright?

Sneha: I am okay. The medicines they have given for the seizures are really strong, and I get dizzy.

Whenever I take them. The doctors are saying that for my current condition, these are necessary. Let's see if I make it through alive, hehe. So if we were in a relationship, why did we break up?

Me: You will obviously make it through. Don't worry, everything will be fine. It was actually a very short relationship, and over that, it was a long distance too. So... You know how these things are. I got dumped by you. Leave it; it doesn't matter now; it was a long time ago. Tell me how uncle and aunt are now.

Sneha: Mom and Dad are okay. Mom always scolds me for eating medicine. Every day she keeps saying that I am a careless girl and that a five-year-old is more responsible than me. This is not fair; she should not treat me like that. I don't like that.

Me: It's ok. Don't worry. She is your mom. She only scolds you because she cares about you. And trust me, you always had the habit of forgetting to take your medicines on time. If she stops scolding you, I know you won't take your medicines on time.

Sneha: Oh, hello, Mr. I always take my medicines on time. You don't know me, ok?

By the way, did I break your heart when we broke up? Was our breakup tough for you?.

Me: What? Why would you say that? What happened to you all of a sudden?

Sneha: Because you are avoiding answering questions about the relationship. Did I hurt you or do something wrong? Tell me; I want to know.

Me: No, Sneha. You did not do anything wrong. It was just that our breakup was very sudden for me. So I just panicked a little bit at that time. That's all. Nothing more.

Sneha: You know what? I think I did something wrong. And this epilepsy is the price that I will have to pay for it. Sorry again, Rohit.

Me: No, dear, it's nothing like that. Don't overstress too much. Ah, I am actually getting a call from my manager. So, I will have to take that. We'll talk later, then. Just take care.

Sneha: Oh..ok. You too. Bye

I disconnected the call. I sat there, blank. My right hand was searching for my pocket to keep my phone. And my left arm was covered in a sleeve that was drenched in tears.

You know it's easy to brag in front of our friends and curse our exes. By saying thank God, I dodged a bullet. And swear that the person gets hit by a truck. But when anything actually happens to that person, it shakes us to our core. I didn't know what to say or how to react.

Sneha, whom I had adored once, didn't even know who I was now. It was not her fault. But still, it goes without saying that the girl I had loved had forgotten me.

Every memory that I had of us. Lost its meaning in a fraction of a second. It didn't matter anymore. All the close moments that we had shared remained only with me.

And there was nothing that I could do about it. I was only a stranger to her now. And that was the truth, which was staring me in the eyes.

None of the motivational speeches, books, or novels could have prepared me for what had happened. But it was that day that I realised how fragile our memories are.

We tend to be possessive of the people that we love and care about. Saying things like this is my best friend. This is my boyfriend, and I want to live with him for the rest of my life. This is my wife. These are my parents. But in truth, all we have of them, or what connects us to them, are just some neurological connections or memories. Which can vanish in one-tenth of a second, and then whatever time of our lives we have spent with them and the bond that we have with them will just cease to exist.

See, I don't mean to dishearten you by saying that feelings and memories with your loved ones are fragile and you should not pay much attention to them. All I am saying is that you should learn to appreciate them while you have them. Whether we like it or not. In life, there are no retakes for anything. I guess life is unfair to everyone, and this is the only thing that makes it fair.

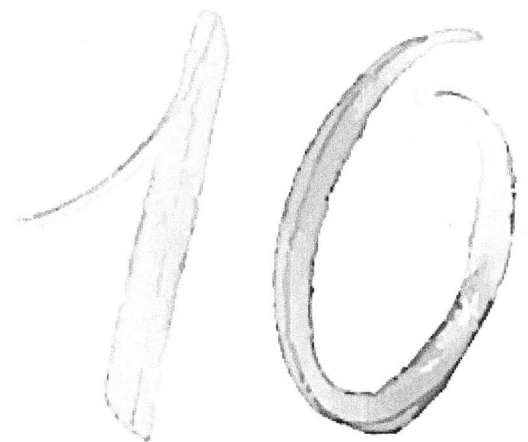

You know, I could have pretended to be cool and unaffected. Sneha was no longer a part of my life, and so it didn't matter to me much what happened to her. And most of it would've been true. My life would be unaffected by what had happened to her. But the real truth was that I was impacted. Not on a physical level. But rather on an emotional and psychological level. I just became numb emotionally, as nothing after that would have happened to me could have, at any level, come on par with Sneha's thing.

I guess it's human nature that once you have seen or faced something bad, You become immune to it. And things that are not as bad as the things you have faced won't affect you that much.

For some time, it seemed as if I had become a shell of my former self.

Till the time we are alive, we will keep getting hurt and then emerge stronger after that; this is just how we are made.

My mentor once said, "Time levels everything up. Be it a crater or a mountain, both come to become plain in the end. And you cannot move into your future until you have made peace with your past."

For me, it took everything that I had to process the situation with Sneha and come to peace with it. There was nothing that I could do that would have changed things. And I had to accept this fact, whether I liked it or not.

Sneha, after this, earned my respect, as even though she had to be rushed to the hospital, many times due to her seizures and was in indescribable pain. She held on strong. She never let any of it get to her, and she kept that jolly nature and cute smile of hers intact.

She proved to be a strong woman through and through.

To my realisation, my part in Sneha's life had come to an end. We lived in different cities, and because of our schedules, it was not possible to meet. I was only a stranger now, and I could only watch her move on in her life from a distance. Some parts of me still cared for her. That one part still hoped for some miracle to happen, and I wished I could just once look her in the eye and tell her how special she was for me. Had this been a movie, this would have also come true. But sadly, it wasn't. Nothing was going to change, whether I liked it or not.

I had reached a point where I just couldn't put any more effort into trying to be with her or just forgetting her for good. In one of our conversations after we first talked, I found out that she was dating someone and that she liked him too. I felt jealous of that guy. But I understood that I had no right to control or interfere in her life or with whom she chose to be with. So I decided to tell her that we needed to stop talking to each other.

I didn't want to beat around the bush, so I just said to her:

"Listen, Just because you don't remember doesn't mean it never happened. I still care for you, and maybe some part of me will keep hoping to get back with you. But we both know that it is not going to happen. So I think it's better that we stop talking. To be clear, I don't hate you or anything like that; it's just that these feelings that I have been ignoring for now need to be dealt with. And for that, I'll have to be away from you. So it's better that you live your life and I live mine. And maybe one day, when I am not expecting that click from you. Then we can be friends again, I guess. Just take care. Bye".

She replied, "Hmm, ok. Whatever makes you feel better. Just don't take much pressure.".

This emotional ride has been tough. But the good thing is that I found myself on this journey. Because of her, I found out how strong I am and that I can be happy with myself.

Now, I am not trying to rush into things. Just take one day at a time. It's peaceful now; I have other things to focus on. Now I can see my life lying ahead of me, waiting to be explored.

It has been 5 years since that day, and I can now say that I have moved on. I got to know that she was getting married soon. At first, I thought that whenever I heard this news, I'd be devastated. But surprisingly, the opposite happened. I felt glad and relieved. And I just felt happy for her. I am no longer the person I once was, I guess. Now I am having fun in my life, and I met some great people along the way. I learned to accept myself for who I am and have been working on myself. I also learned to accept things for what they are. Overall, it has been fun.

I just want to say that in life things happen, people come and go. It never gets easier; we just become tough. But that's the fun part. What happened to me—some might say it was good, and some might say it was bad.

But I don't think either way. I just think of it as an experience that I had to go through. It helped make me who I am today. There was nothing good, bad, happy, or sad about it.

This was just it, only a part of my life...

Made in the USA
Monee, IL
03 May 2026

49438461R00052